COME INTO THE LION'S DEN AND MEET...

Agnes
Christian girl

Cass
A trainee animal keeper at the Flavian Amphitheatre in Rome

mmodus
A training to be a gladiator

Lucilla
The Emperor's daughter

A lion w reath

Black Cats

The Ramsbottom Rumble • Georgia Byng
Calamity Kate • Terry Deary
The Custard Kid • Terry Deary
The Ghosts of Batwing Castle • Terry Deary
Ghost Town • Terry Deary
Into the Lion's Den • Terry Deary
The Joke Factory • Terry Deary
The Treasure of Crazy Horse • Terry Deary
The Wishing Well Ghost • Terry Deary
A Witch in Time • Terry Deary
Dear Ms • Joan Poulson
It's a Tough Life • Jeremy Strong
Big Iggy • Kaye Umansky
Something Slimy on Primrose Drive • Karen Wallace

First published 2002 by
A & C Black Publishers Ltd
37 Soho Square, London W1D 3QZ
www.acblack.com

Text copyright © 2002 Terry Deary
Illustrations copyright © 2002 Lynne Chapman

The rights of Terry Deary and Lynne Chapman to be identified as
author and illustrator of this work have been asserted by them
in accordance with the Copyrights, Designs and Patents Act 1988.

ISBN 0-7136-6189-5

A CIP catalogue for this book is available from the British Library.

A & C Black uses paper produced with elemental
chlorine-free pulp, harvested from managed sustainable forests.

Printed and bound in Spain by G. Z. Printek, Bilbao.

INTO THE LION'S DEN

TERRY DEARY

ILLUSTRATED BY
LYNNE CHAPMAN

A & C BLACK • LONDON

CHAPTER ONE
Letter from a lion's dinner

The girl placed the scroll of paper on the floor. She let the light from the candle fall onto it and she began to write…

Dear Uncle Paul,

Today I'm going to be eaten by a lion. They tell me it will be quick. One snap of the lion's jaw and I'll go out like an oil lamp in a storm. Then I'll wake up at the gates of Heaven.

But I'm not sure. I mean – I've seen cats catch mice. They play with them and shake them and let them run and catch them. Lions are just like big cats, aren't they? What if the lion picks me up and shakes me? That'll hurt! And what if it lets me run? I wonder if I should?

Of course, the crowd would love that, wouldn't they? Once I'm in the arena the gates are barred behind me and the fences are too high to climb. I can run, but there's nowhere to run to. It would catch me in the end.

I share my prison with Miriam, a Christian lady. I asked Miriam what I should do and she said, "Just lie on your face in the sand and feel the warm. Close your eyes, and stretch out your arms so you make the shape of a cross. Then forget about the lion. Think of Jesus and pray. Tell him you'll be seeing him soon and it will be the happiest day of your life!"

I have to tell you Uncle, I don't feel very happy!

Pray for me.

Your loving niece, Agnes

Miriam sat in the corner of the cell. She was old enough to be Agnes's mother. Her wavy hair was long and tangled and wild as a thorn bush.

She sat next to old Balbus (who was old enough to be Agnes's grandfather), a man with eyes as pale as water and white-feather hair. Miriam took a scrap of paper from the old man's trembling hands and her eager eyes raced across the words.

'What is it?' Agnes asked.

'It's a miracle! It's the work of brother Balbus here!' Miriam told her.

'But what is it?' Agnes asked. 'It's not an escape plan?'

'No! It's a hymn!'

'Him? Who's him?'

'Brother Balbus's hymn, a *hymn* of praise! Brother Balbus wants us to learn it and sing it when we go out to face the lions. We will march out, heads held high and happy! Show the people we aren't afraid to die!' the woman went on excitedly.

'But I *am* afraid to die!' Agnes said quietly.

'This will give you courage,' Miriam told her, waving the paper. 'Look. Let's practise together.' Miriam's strong but tuneless voice rang out like a bell struck against the cool, damp walls of the cell. Agnes joined in with a softer, trembling tone while Balbus warbled to a different tune altogether...

All things bright and wonderful,
All creatures like the lion,
All things cruel and terrible
We ain't afraid of dyin'!

But if you're listening lion,
We have a nice suggestion,
Don't you eat us Christians
Or you'll get indigestion!

All things bright and wonderful,
We are your daily bread.
But if you eat us Christians
You won't get into Heaven
when you're dead.

By Balbus the Brave.

Miriam went on, 'Oh, brother Balbus, what a great man you are!'

'A great man!' said Agnes.

'Oh, brother Balbus, what a great scholar you are!'

'A great scholar… but a rotten poet,' Agnes shrugged.

Miriam glared at her, 'That's unkind, sister Agnes. You should not be preparing yourself for Heaven by being so unkind.'

Miriam shook her head. 'I just meant, it sounds to me as if brother Balbus doesn't *want* to die! *You* want the lion to eat us, sister Miriam... Balbus's hymn says he *doesn't*. Who am I supposed to believe?'

Miriam turned to the deaf old man and shook the paper under his nose, 'You... want... the... lion... to... eat... us?' she shouted.

Balbus showed pink gums in a toothless smile. 'I'm not lying?'

'No, not lying... lion!' Miriam shouted.

'Dying? Yes, lion dying to eat us!' Balbus nodded.

'What's on the back of the hymn?' Agnes asked.

The girl turned it over and clutched at her throat in fear. It was a timetable for the day.

Ninth hour of the morning:
    Comic fights with wooden swords
    A battle between a lion and a tiger
    A battle between a bear and a bull

Tenth hour of the morning:
    Trained animal performances
    A lion catching a hare without killing it
    A performing elephant

Eleventh hour of the morning:
    Animals against men
    A man armed with a net against a crocodile
    A man armed with a sword against a panther
    An unarmed man against a bear

Noon:
    Execution of criminals
    Execution of Christians and other trouble-makers
    by various animals
    A drama in which a criminal will be chained to
    a rock like Orpheus and attacked by bears

First hour of the afternoon:
    Gladiators against gladiators

Second hour of the afternoon:
    Gladiators against animals

Third hour of the afternoon:
    Lottery
    The Emperor will throw out wooden balls
    Prizes from cakes to a block of flats

'I wish I could win a cake in the lottery,' Agnes said simply.

'You'll be dead before then,' Miriam said without thinking.

The girl's eyes pricked with tears and they trickled down and splashed on the floor. 'Noon. We die at noon.'

'Four hours,' Miriam said.

'Cold showers?' Balbus creaked. 'No cold showers out there. It's going to be hot today.'

'Poor old man,' Agnes said quietly. 'If we hadn't been shouting the Lord's Prayer for brother Balbus, that soldier would never have heard us and caught us last Sunday.'

'We should be glad he did,' Miriam said.

'We were just unlucky,' the girl argued.

'Emperor Marcus Aurelius doesn't care much about Christians. He only executes the ones his soldiers catch.'

Balbus seemed to hear her. 'The feller that caught us wasn't a soldier!' he croaked.

'He was wearing armour,' Miriam reminded him.

'He's a feller they call Metal-head! He runs the gladiator school! I reckon he was short of people to execute today, so he picked on us. Big day today!'

'Why?' Miriam asked.

'Aye!' Balbus nodded.

'No, brother Balbus… she said 'Why?'… why is today a big day?' Agnes said in her clear high voice that the old man seemed to hear better.

'Because the Emperor's coming today. He's bringing his young daughter for the first time. The people want to see the lass. Lady Lucilla, they call her.'

'Loose sinner of a girl,' Miriam spat.

'That's what I said,' Balbus nodded. 'Lucilla!'

Agnes clutched at her letter. 'Will that guard come back? The one who promised to take my letter to my Uncle Paul?'

Miriam shrugged. 'You never know in this place. Put your uncle's name on the front and say that the person who takes it will be paid. Some greedy heathen is bound to take it.'

Agnes bent over the letter and began to write the address. The letters were smudged as the tears splashed onto it.

CHAPTER TWO
Orders for a lion keeper

Cass walked into the dark doorway and the sour-sweet, foul-filth smell hit him like a fist. He'd liked animals before he came here to work at the Amphitheatre. He didn't mind mucking out the stables of the family donkey and the horse droppings in the streets never bothered him.

But this smell was the smell of meat-eaters and it made the boy just a little sick. Then there was the constant grumbling and rumbling of the snarling beasts, the baring of teeth when he walked past the cages and the dull hatred in the animals' eyes.

'You're late!' the fat and greasy animal keeper growled.

His name was Ferox, a name that Romans gave to their dogs. The boy bit his lip to stop himself from laughing nervously. Ferox the dog was just like the animals he looked after: threatening, hateful… and just as smelly.

'There were guards on the gate,' Cass explained. 'The streets are packed with tents of people who've come to see the games and the executions.'

'Aye, there would be. The Emperor's coming today. Likes to see a bit of blood spilt does the Emperor,' the keeper chuckled then his flat nose curled a little. 'So long as it's not his own blood,' he muttered and looked as sly-eyed as the alligator behind him.

'Has the Emperor got blood?' Cass asked, wide-eyed.

'Uh? 'Course he has!'

'But he's a god, isn't he? He can't be killed, can he?' the boy persisted.

'We'll see,' the keeper murmured into his greasy tunic, so quietly that Cass didn't think he heard right.

'Now, you know what to do, boy?' the keeper said, breathing his foul breath into Cass's face.

He was so close Cass could see the bits of meat stuck between his teeth.

'Yes. You showed me yesterday.'

'Well, I've had one of the scribes write it down.

You're a clever little son of a rat, aren't you? You can *read*, can't you?' he asked, waving a scroll of parchment under the boy's nose.

'Yes, sir! And I've learned numbers.'

'Well, read that,' he said and smacked his young helper round the head with the scroll then let it fall onto the slimy stone of the floor.

Cass unrolled it and read…

The Noon Executions

1 Animal: Lion – Max
Criminals: Agnes the Christian
Miriam the Christian
Balbus the Christian

2 Animal: Bear – Bruno
Criminal: Thrysus the runaway slave.
Chained to rock.

Ferox jabbed a finger at the paper. 'You understand it?'

'Yes, Ferox.'

'I'll be in charge of the bear – you'll have to look after the lion and the Christians.'

'Me?'

'Yes,' Ferox snarled. 'That's what you're here for. I showed you what to do yesterday. When they give the signal you open the gate and let the lion, Max, out into the arena.'

'What if it tries to attack me?' Cass asked.

'You'll be armed.'

'With a sword and armour like the gladiators?' the boy asked hopefully.

'With a whip,' Ferox told him.

'Oh.'

The man pointed to a plan on the wall...

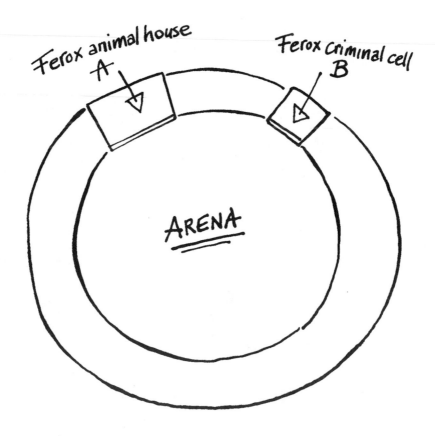

'You leave the lion in the arena – the people like to get a good look at the beasts before they do their killing – then you open the prisoners' cell door that leads out into the arena.'

'What if the prisoners attack me?' Cass asked.

'You have your whip,' Ferox sneered. 'Anyway, there's only an old man, a woman and a girl. They won't give you any trouble. May try to do a bit of singing. Just smack them with the whip if they do. Anyway, push them in with the lion and lock the arena door behind them.'

'And then I'm finished?'

'No. The slaves will drag what's left of the Christians out through the doors here,' the animal keeper said tapping the plan. 'You'll walk into the arena and get the lion back into his cage.'

'With my whip?'

'No problem, boy. By the time he's crunched three Christians the lion won't be hungry enough to trouble you... oh, and that reminds me! Don't let Max get near any food *before* he eats the Christians. Understand? He's been starved for three days to keep him hungry and angry.'

Cass nodded.

'Attendants do sometimes get eaten by the animals, of course!' Ferox said cheerfully. 'And I've heard that Emperor Claudius was once so annoyed with one attendant that he had the man thrown to his own panthers! Hah!

You'd better hope that doesn't happen to you, boy!'

'No,' Cass said. His mouth was dry with fear.

'Go and look at the lion's dinner,' Ferox said.

'What?'

'Check on the prisoners! Those trumpets you hear are the signal they're about to start. I have to get a bull taken out for the sacrifice. Keep busy.'

'Yes, Ferox.'

'And here!' the animal keeper said, grabbing the boy by the shoulder of his tunic. 'When they sacrifice the bull I'll make sure there's a nice leg from the beast to feed us. The slaves will carve a piece off before they drag it off.'

'Thanks, Ferox.'

Cass walked down the gloomy corridor. The noises of the angry animals were mingled with the excited chatter of the crowds as the doors opened and they were let in. Fifty thousand feet rumbled up the stairways. Cushion-men at the doors cried, 'Cushions for rent! Cushions for rent! Try my cushions – six hours on a stone seat will numb your bum! Cushions for rent!'

Cass reached the door of the cell and paused. He heard muttering female voices. 'It's him. It's the nice young guard. Slip him your letter now. It'll be your last chance!'

Suddenly a folded sheet of paper slid under the door. The address in childish lettering said...

To Paul the Doctor
via Maximus
Rome

Cass unfolded the sheet and read the girl's letter. The girl he would push to her death in three hours' time. He smelled her fear, as real as the scent of the animals.

The boy slid back the bolt on the door and opened it. The dark-haired, wide-eyed girl and the skinny woman with the gap-toothed grin looked at him. Their eyes moved down to the letter in his hand.

'You're not the nice young guard,' Miriam said.

'No, I'm an animal keeper. This letter—'

'Is harmless!' Agnes said quickly. 'A last letter to my uncle! Please see it's delivered!'

Cass pushed it into the belt of his tunic and started to close the door.

'Who'll do it?' Agnes cried.

'Do what?' Cass asked.

'Throw us to the lion?' the girl moaned.

Cass couldn't look her in the eye. 'I don't know,' he lied. 'It depends… who's on duty.'

He shut the door quickly and ran back to the animal cages. Max stared at him with a burning, hungry hatred and curled back his nose when Cass stretched out a hand towards him and spoke through the bars. 'Not long, Max. Three hours and you'll have all the food you can eat – they're poor skinny things, but there are three of them.'

Max snarled, ran a tongue over yellow teeth and licked his lips.

CHAPTER THREE
Report on a great gladiator

The man with the leather armour leaned across the table and gave the bald man in a toga a grim smile. 'What we need is someone to cause an uproar in the amphitheatre! Someone who will drive the crowd so wild that no one will notice what we're up to.' The man's armour creaked as he sat back.

The bald man in the toga had a face as thin as the east wind and a nose as sharp and curved as a battleaxe. 'Is there anyone in gladiator school who could do that?' he asked. He was Senator Verres, known to his enemies in Rome as 'Vicious Verres'. (No one knew what his friends called him because he didn't have any.)

'We have someone in the gladiator school who could cause chaos in a cemetery. If we let him loose the corpses would jump from their graves and run away.' The man in armour tapped the parchment scroll in front of him. When he grinned, the criss-cross of old sword wounds creased his face deeply. He was Metellus, the head of the gladiator's school. His pupils (and the teachers who worked for him) called him 'Metal-head', because he was never seen without his helmet. Too many people hated him, too many people would stab him in the back – or the front or the side – if they had a whisker of a chance.

'This boy is a walking disaster, senator. Read his report.'

The thin man in the toga unrolled the report and read…

GLADIATOR SCHOOL REPORT ✕

STUDENT: Commodus

<u>Family</u> ～
This boy is well-born, but that must be kept secret. He must be treated like the child of a freeman, but not the child of a slave. He must fight with a wooden practice sword at all times and not risk injury with real swords.

<u>Skills</u> ～
The boy is keen. Sadly his hands don't always go where his mind wants them to… or his feet. In short, he's a clumsy oaf. Still we have tried to train him in the different gladiator skills, with mixed results.

I RETARIUS: (fighting with a net and a trident spear). He managed to throw the net at his opponent quite smoothly ~ sadly he then ran forward too quickly and the net landed on his own head and he entangled himself.

FAILED

II SECUTOR: (armed with a sword and shield, with armour on his sword arm – usually fights against a Retarius). Commodus proved to be a very dangerous Secutor. He missed the Retarius with his sword swing and nearly killed his teacher. (With a real sword the teacher's head would still have been rolling towards the river).

FAILED

III BESTARIUS: (armed with spear, sword and dagger, set to kill dangerous wild animals in the arena). Didn't seem to understand that you do not go up to a panther and say, "Here, pussy pussy." And you don't go up to a crocodile and say, "My! What a big mouth you've got!" (Luckily the school animals had their teeth blunted).

FAILED

IV VENATO: (hunting wild animals in a forest). Got lost.

FAILED

V DIMACHERIUS: (fighting armed with two swords).

Very interesting and terrifying to watch Commodus fight with two swords. The swords whirled like a wasp's wings. The opponent was unharmed but Commodus managed to turn his tunic to shreds and cut his own hair.

FAILED

VI LAQUEATORUS: (fighting with a rope noose).

Failed to catch any animals or gladiators with the noose, but he did catch a tree. Somehow the rope ended round his neck and he had to be cut down before he hanged himself.

FAILED

Summary~

Commodus is a very dangerous young man. He is a danger to his teachers, to the animal keepers and most of all, to himself. The hospital is full of Commodus's little 'accidents'. If he is ever fit to fight in an arena, I will eat my toga. We have never had a pupil like Commodus in this school, and I hope we never have again!

Report by Instructor Martial

The senator leaned back and smiled. 'Perfect. Quite perfect!'

Metal-head said, 'The lad's just out of hospital himself. Put a helmet on the wrong way round and walked into a door! Hah!'

'No serious damage, I hope?' Vicious Verres frowned.

'Damage! He didn't just splinter the door – he wrecked the hinges and the doorframe, too!'

'I meant no damage to his head.'

Metal-head looked up to the cloudless morning sky. 'Senator, his head is harder than any helmet I've ever seen. Commodus just scratched his nose. Now, are we ready to see him?'

Vicious Verres gave a nod like the chop of an axe. Metellus bellowed towards the door, 'Send in Commodus!'

There was a rattle and a clatter and a boy walked in. He wasn't very old but he was fat and quite tall for his age. He grinned at the two men.

'Good morning, gents.'

'Sir!' Metellus growled. 'You are supposed to call me 'sir'!'

'But I'm the—' the boy began.

'We know who you are… but it's a secret! Your father has a lot of enemies. If those enemies knew you were here they'd…' Metal-head stopped suddenly. 'What's that in your hand, boy?'

Commodus's grin turned into a huge smile.

'Sorry… sir… it's the door handle. It just sort of came away in my hand. They don't have very good handles in this school, do they?'

Metellus took a deep breath and his sun-tanned face turned brick red with anger.

The senator touched him lightly on the wrist and spoke up, 'Commodus,' he said. 'We have a report here from your teachers.'

'Ohhhh! Have I passed?' the boy asked.

'Passed?' Vicious Verres said smoothly. 'The instructor says, 'We have never had a pupil like Commodus in this school.''

'That good, eh?' Commodus said and puffed out his fat chest.

'The teachers have seen no one like you!'

Commodus spread his hands. It was meant to show his modesty, but the door handle he'd forgotten he'd been holding flew out of his open hand and clanged against the helmet of Metellus.

'Oops! Does that mean I get the chance to fight in the amphitheatre?'

'You do. We were just saying you'll be perfect!' Verres said softly.

'Great! My dad'll be there today to see me! And my sister! They'll be so proud of me – and I'll be so proud of me! Great!' the boy grinned. 'What will I be today? Retarius? Secutor?'

Metellus rubbed at the dent in his helmet and said crossly, 'Neither. We have something very special for you. You're going to be part of a new show that we have planned. The crowds have been getting bored and restless with all the simple blood and the killing. We have something totally new planned for you.'

'Great!' Commodus sighed happily. 'Great... sir!'

CHAPTER FOUR
Diary of a lovely lady

Lucilla rose from her bed and her hand-maidens were waiting. The girl was small but held her back straight and her head high so she looked like a goddess... which she had decided she was anyway.

'Prepare my bath,' she snapped at one slave-girl. 'My finest robe with the golden threads,' she said to another. 'And bring me breakfast,' she told a third. To the fourth she said, 'I will sit by my window to write my diary this morning.'

She sat on a purple silken cushion and looked out over the scented gardens of the Emperor's palace. The sun was warm already. The noise of the crowds in the city drifted up to her. She wrinkled her nose as if she could smell the peasants in the crowded streets.

'Now take this down,' she ordered the bright-eyed girl with the pen and parchment...

Today I go to the Amphitheatre for the first time. Oh, but I do so look forward to it. Fifty thousand people will be there to see me and wonder at my beauty. Oh those lucky lucky Roman people.

And oh, the excitement of the shows I'll see there! But I do wish there could be more Christians for the lions to eat. Father is so lazy about finding those dreadful people. They bury their dead in corridors under the ground - catacombs, they call them. They drink the blood of their Jesus in one of their services - but of course, they don't really have his blood. I have heard they murder children and drink their blood instead. They are cannibals and deserve to die.

But, most disgusting of all, they refuse to call my father a god! A hundred years ago the Emperor Nero blamed the Christians for the great fire of Rome. He killed thousands of them! He covered them in animal skins so they'd be torn apart by packs of hungry dogs. That's what I'd do too, if I had my way.

I have heard that today there are just three miserable Christians to be executed. And not even strong men who will put up an exciting fight! Just some feeble girl, some wild woman and a wrinkled old man. Still if the crowds get bored they can always look at me.

And my brother has just come to my room, full of excitement! The mad boy simply wants to be a gladiator. Those brutal slaves and common men are disgusting but that's what he wants to be! Criminals are sent to be gladiators - it's like a death sentence. Most will be dead within the year. There is just a chance that they may fight bravely and the crowd at the amphitheatre may call for the man to be set free. And useless slaves or enemies of war may become gladiators. For the son of the Emperor to choose to become a gladiator is just too shocking. Why, he's my brother and I am almost a goddess!

Anyway, Metellus, the head of the gladiator school, said my brother could fight in a special show of his own today. Of course, my father would be furious if he knew! He only lets my brother fight with wooden swords and against animals with blunted teeth. If he knew his dear son was going to fight real wild animals, his sick stomach would burst on the spot!

My brother has seen many shows before, of course. I've never been allowed. That's not fair. He says the gladiators arrive in chariots. They're dressed in purple cloaks with golden threads. When they see Father, they cry, "Hail to the Emperor! The men who are about to die salute you!" Of course, only half of them die.

Then the gladiators fight — with wooden swords at first, for fun, then to the death. But at noon the criminals are thrown to the wild beasts. The Emperor doesn't usually stay to watch that, but I want to! I will tell father he has to! Father always does what I want.

After the animal has killed the criminals, then a gladiator kills the animal! They say a lion called Max is to be the animal chosen today. He'll

have been starved for three days.
Great Jupiter, I couldn't go for three
hours!

That reminds me, I must stop now
for breakfast. Pears from Syria this
morning, with a little watered wine
from Greece.

What a truly wonderful day for
the people of Rome. To see the lovely
Lucilla at last! I must use my finest
face powders and brush my hair till it
shines like a chestnut!

Lucilla waved her scribe away and went to her
heated bath house. She returned to have her hair
brushed and fastened back in a fine net of gold.
'Owww!' she cried as the ivory comb was drawn
through her fine hair.

The old matron in charge of the slave-girls
hurried across to Lucilla, sitting in her cedarwood
chair. 'Was something wrong, your grace?'

Lucilla's nostrils were wide and red. 'This... this
clumsy slave... hurt the head of the goddess
Lucilla!' she cried.

'There was a tangle…' the slave-girl began. She didn't finish.

'Have her taken into the courtyard, stripped to the waist and whipped with a cane twenty times!' Lucilla ordered. As the quivering girl was led to the door the Emperor's daughter called, 'Make sure it is a thin cane so it stings the way her careless combing stung my scalp! And don't forget to wait till I come to the window to watch!'

The Emperor came into the room, 'Aren't you ready, Lucilla? The crowds are filling the streets. We'll be late if you don't hurry!'

The girl looked at her father. He clutched at his stomach. It always gave him pain when he was tense. He was a thin, sour-faced man with fine hair combed forward and curled to cover his baldness.

'Father, I haven't had my hair combed!' Lucilla told him.

'Then get your girl to do it!' he groaned.

'I can't!'

'Why not?'

'Because I'm having her beaten!'

'Then hurry, my girl! Hurry! Just like your mother. Never ready on time. Oh, my grumbling guts!' He turned and walked out of the room.

Lucilla walked lazily to the window. 'Quickly! Beat her quickly and get her back up here as soon as you can!' she called down.

Before Lucilla had finished her third pear the snivelling slave-girl was back, combing carefully while a second slave powdered her lady's face with chalk. She dusted crushed red ochre rock onto the cheeks and lips then smoothed ashes onto the eyelids.

Lucilla looked at herself in the silver mirror and wondered what was wrong. The face she saw scowled back at her. Lucilla smiled. The face smiled and looked the most beautiful thing she had ever seen.

'Lucky Roman people,' she sighed. She clicked her fingers. 'Have a carrying chair brought to the door for me. Tell my father I am ready!'

Slaves hurried to obey her and in moments four massive slaves stood holding a chair framed with curtains. Lucilla stepped in and the slaves picked it up. The Emperor came fussing through the door. 'Your brother? Where's your brother?'

'I think he said we'll see him there,' the girl said with a secret smile.

A squadron of guards surrounded the chairs and they were carried quickly out into the dusty streets. People scattered when they saw them coming. The ones who didn't were kicked out of the way by the armoured legs of the guards or swatted with the flat of their short swords.

The Emperor's daughter climbed a dozen steps up to the richly cushioned seats at the front of the amphitheatre. Lucilla blinked in the brilliant morning sun that glared through a striped canopy. At least that shaded them from the worst of the heat. Smoke from sweet-perfumed wood scented the air and took away the stench of the animals below. The crowd of thousands was quickly hushed.

The Emperor walked out below onto the fresh, golden sand of the arena.

All eyes turned towards him.

He raised a hand and called, 'Let the games begin!'

There was a sudden roar of sound, as if a dam had burst, when the crowd began cheering. Gates opened and chariots entered, carrying the gladiators. They walked in a slow line behind the Emperor.

The games would soon begin. The first games for Lucilla.

The last games for some who waited below in the damp dark.

CHAPTER FIVE
A plea to an animal keeper

Old Balbus looked around the bleak, grey cell. 'I helped to build places like this!' he said suddenly.

'You did?' Agnes said. She was glad to have something to talk about to take her mind off the screaming crowds above and the thought of noon.

'Yes, I was a slave before I earned my freedom,' the old man smiled gently.

'So you know the plan of this amphitheatre?' Agnes asked. 'You could guide us to the way out?'

But Balbus was remembering. 'I was as strong as one of those elephants they have in here!'

'What's an elephant?' Miriam asked.

'A great grey monster with a nose like a snake and two horns on its face. They're as tall as a house!' he explained. He took the pen and ink pot from Agnes and did a drawing for the women on the back of a poster that was lying around.

'They put sharp iron spikes here on the end of the horns,' he went on. 'That's so two bull elephants can fight each other to the death.'

'Poor creatures,' Agnes sighed.

'And ostriches!' Balbus said, shaking his head. 'If you think elephants are strange, you should see the ostriches.'

'Are they like crocodiles?' Agnes asked. 'I've seen a crocodile.'

'No, no, no! Ostriches are giant birds. They've got long legs and even longer necks. They can give you a nasty peck can ostriches.'

'And they fight?' Miriam asked.

'No, no! They send archers into the arena. These archers have arrows with wide blades on the end. The trick is to hit the ostrich bird in the neck and slice its head clean off! The headless bodies go on running for ages! The crowds love that. Of course, if the arrow flies into the crowd it could kill someone!'

'Serve them right,' Agnes muttered.

Miriam's wide eyes looked shocked. 'We are all God's creatures, girl. Even the Romans. We must learn to forgive our enemies. You mustn't have hatred in your heart. Not now when you're about to die!'

Agnes stood up, furious. 'Miriam, for the love of Jesus, stop saying that!'

'Agnes, child! You mustn't swear on our Lord's name like that!' the woman cried. 'Our Lord who died so we might live!'

Agnes gave a harsh laugh. 'We aren't *going* to live, though, *are* we? Unless we get out of here!'

'Get out?'

'Yes! Balbus here has built places like this. He must know where the passages lead. If we can get that guard boy to unbolt the door, then we can get away! Give me the pen, Balbus!' Agnes said.

The girl took the last scrap of poster and began to write…

Dear friend,

I am sorry I don't know your name. I think you don't want to see us die. You are a boy no older than me. We are harmless people, an old freedman, a lonely woman and a girl who could be your sister. Do you have a sister? Our deaths would entertain the people for a few moments and feed a lion, but they would do no one any good.

But, if you helped us to live, then your goodness would be remembered by our God forever more. I know you're not a Christian, but even the Roman gods love brave men. You would have to be very brave to leave the door to our cell open.

You have to believe me, we are harmless. Those stories about us eating flesh and drinking blood are nonsense. We eat bread and drink wine in memory of our Lord's flesh and blood. And we refuse to call the Emperor a god, but we still obey him in every other way.

I don't want to die brother. You can save me,

Agnes

The girl folded the letter and walked across to the door. Miriam sniffed. 'He probably can't read,' she said.

Agnes stopped. 'No... I handed him the letter for my uncle. He looked at the address and he didn't have to ask me what it was. He can read!'

'He probably wants to see you torn apart by the lion anyway,' Miriam said and she made her bony hands snatch at the air like claws.

Agnes hammered on the door. 'Hello!'

'They're all too busy,' Miriam told her. 'Now the games have started they'll be rushing backwards and forwards. You'd be much better off spending your time praying,' she said.

Agnes hammered again, 'Hello!'

'Hello!' Balbus called back cheerfully. 'Is it our turn to go in already?' he asked.

'No, Balbus, I'm calling for help!'

'They'll all be too busy,' said the old man.

Miriam chuckled, 'That's exactly what I've just told her!'

'Be bolder?' Balbus said, holding a hand up to his ear. 'Yes, the lass will have to be bolder. Sing that hymn I wrote!' he cried and set off with a tuneless roar.

The door bolt rattled and a fat, ugly man stood there. His filthy hands were stained with blood and his sweating face was angry. 'Shut up, you stupid old fool!'

Balbus smiled at him. 'Hello, brother!'

'I'm not your brother. My name is Ferox, head animal keeper. And if you don't shut up I'll feed you to the lion one piece at a time!'

He turned on Agnes, who stood there shocked and frightened. 'What you got there?' he asked.

Too late she swept the poster behind her back. He grabbed her arm and savagely snatched the paper from her. 'What's this?'

'Nothing,' Agnes whispered.

'It's got writing on it,' Ferox spat. 'What does it say then?'

'You can see,' Agnes mumbled. Her mouth was dry. When Ferox read it then her hope of escape was finished and the boy could die along with them. The letter was a horrible mistake.

Ferox jabbed a grimy finger at her shoulder. 'Yes, I can *see*, my little Christian lion's lunch – but I can't *read* it, can I? I hate the way you Christians are so clever. Same as that new attendant boy!' His face was turning purple with rage. 'So you can *read?* So *what?* So it won't do you much good out in the arena. What you going to do then, eh? Write a little letter to Max the lion? 'Dear Max, you'll never get to lion heaven if you eat me?' Hah! Let's see if your clever-clever reading and writing can save your miserable lives!'

The animal keeper crumpled the paper and threw it out of the door. He was panting with the effort of shouting. 'Next time you see Ferox I'll be dragging what's left of you out of the arena. I'll be putting your remains on a cart and sending you off to some pit to be buried. Let's see what good your writing can do you then, eh?'

Miriam rose to her feet and spread her arms. 'Ferox, you are my hero!' she cried and rushed towards him. She hugged him.

The animal keeper staggered back. 'Here! Cut that out! I'm a married man!'

'You will throw me to the lion that will lead me to my heaven!'

He wriggled and struggled but her hands like talons were fastened to his tunic sleeves. 'Get off, you mad witch!'

'You're my brother and I love you!' she cried.

'You're not my sister and I hate you!' he squawked and tore himself free. He stumbled backwards towards the door. 'You'll be better off dead!'

'Oh, I *will!*' Miriam cried. 'I *will!*' She took a step towards him. Ferox turned and ran. He swung the door shut behind him.

In his haste he didn't bolt it.

CHAPTER SIX
A plot against an Emperor

Ferox's face was still a pale shade of purple when he arrived back at the animal pens. Spittle sprayed from his mouth as he hissed at young Cass, 'When that lion goes into the arena, starving, just give him a few flicks from the whip to make him really angry, will you, boy?'

Cass shook his head. 'He's angry enough!'

'Don't argue with me! I want that big cat so furious it will tear those Christians into a hundred pieces. Understand?'

'Why?'

'Don't ask questions, boy! Just *do* it! Do it! Hear me? Do it!'

Cass held up his hands, palms towards the head keeper. 'Yes, sir. I just wondered if there was anything else I could do… to make the lion even more angry,' the boy asked craftily.

Ferox's fat chest was heaving. He gulped the foul air and steadied himself. The man's red-rimmed eyes turned on the boy. 'We have a special plan for today's executions… I suppose I'd better tell you what it is.' Cass just nodded silently and Ferox went on, 'We want to add a drama – a piece of theatre. The lion will go into the arena.

You will push the Christians in and the lion will scent them and go after them. But then we will put in a gladiator, too. The gladiator will look to save the Christians as if he's some great hero come to the rescue! See?' Ferox scratched a circle on the stone floor using the tip of his dagger. He marked each entrance.

'One is the lion, two is the Christians and three is the gladiator.' Suddenly Ferox jabbed a blunt finger at the boy. 'Remember what happens to attendants who get the timing wrong?'

'So will the gladiator save the Christians?' the boy asked hopefully.

Ferox looked sly. 'Hah! That's the point, isn't it? You're interested, aren't you. The Emperor will be interested, too. The whole crowd will want to know what's going to happen.'

Cass shook his head. 'I don't see why that's important.'

Ferox lowered his voice. 'Executions always happen at noon. The Emperor always leaves when the executions begin. Most of the crowd go off to get some lunch. Once our little drama starts then no one will leave, will they? Especially when word gets around who the gladiator is!'

'Who?'

Ferox gave an evil smile and didn't reply for a long moment. 'A young boy from the gladiator school. A boy your age. A boy called Commodus!'

'Commodus!' Cass gasped. 'But that's the name of the Emperor's son!'

Ferox drew as he spoke. 'Yes, just picture it! Suddenly the crowd and the Emperor know that the young Lord Commodus is out there in the arena, facing death! All eyes will be on the arena. The Emperor will panic.

One of the senators called Verres will tell the Emperor what to do!'

'Vicious Verres? Is he the one?'

'He's the one.'

'What *can* the Emperor do?' Cass asked.

'The boy Commodus is the worst pupil ever to go to gladiator school. He will die if no one goes to his rescue. Verres will tell the Emperor there is only one way the boy can be saved in time... the Emperor's bodyguards must jump off the fence and into the arena!'

'Once those guards are in the arena they can't get back up. The Emperor will be unguarded!' Ferox leered.

'So?'

'So... that will be when Verres and Metellus kidnap the Emperor! The plan is perfect. It just can't fail!'

Cass's mouth was dry. 'Why would you want to kidnap Marcus Aurelius, Ferox?'

The animal keeper's nose curled into a sneer. 'Emperor Marcus Aurelius doesn't execute enough Christians. Some powerful men in Rome want to see more done to exterminate them.'

'People like Vicious Verres?' the boy asked.

'Exactly. We'll keep the Emperor safe until he agrees to our demands.'

'And if he doesn't agree?'

'Then he'll end up on an alligator's dinner table and Verres will take over as Emperor. That may not be a bad thing. I would have a very high position under the new Emperor Verres, that's for sure. And you can have my job here! Imagine it, boy! The youngest chief animal keeper ever! And hundreds of Christians – thousands and thousands – to keep you busy and rich!'

Cass was sick at the thought. Especially if they were all as helpless as that girl Agnes and the mad woman and the old man.

'You'll have as many slaves as you want,' Ferox was saying, 'and you'll be the most powerful man in the amphitheatre. Just make sure everything goes right in that arena at noon.'

The gates clattered open and a dead bull was dragged into the corridor. Max the lion sprang to his feet at the smell of the fresh meat and clawed at the bars of the cage till they shook and threatened to snap. Ferox drew his dagger and waved it at the lion. 'Do your job at noon and you'll have all the beef you can eat – unless the Emperor's bodyguard kills you first!'

The man laughed then used the knife to carve off the dead animal's leg. 'That will roast nicely for supper tonight. I think there may just be a party here tonight for Emperor Verres and the gladiators who help him.'

The attendants took the rest of the beast out to the waiting carts outside the amphitheatre. Cass asked, 'You seem sure Verres *will* become Emperor? What about if Marcus Aurelius agrees to exterminate the Christians?'

Ferox wiped his knife on his filthy, stained tunic and refused to meet the boy's gaze. 'Marcus might promise that – but could we trust him to keep his promise?'

'You plan to kill him anyway, don't you?' Cass asked.

Ferox looked at him. 'All right. We plan to kill him. *We*. Don't forget *you're* part of the plot, too, young Cassius!'

Cass opened his mouth but no sound came out. Before Ferox had stormed in Cass was worried about how he could save the Christians. Now he had to think of a way of saving the Emperor, too! It was too much to expect him to save both.

Ferox touched the tip of his knife with his thumb. 'Of course you may decide not to help us. Tell me now and save a lot of trouble. I'll just cut your throat here and now. No one will notice one more body on the gladiator's cart!'

The boy gave a bold smile. 'No, sir! I want your job – I want an army of slaves. You can trust me!' Ferox gave a nod that set his heavy cheeks wobbling. 'I knew I could, boy. I knew I could!'

Cass thought he could hear a faint and distant screech, but it was only his own mind screaming at him. And it was yelling, 'H-e-l-p!'

CHAPTER SEVEN
The gladiator's glory

Metellus was in armour. He slapped an armoured arm around young Commodus's shoulders. The boy gasped with the pain. 'You will be a hero today!' the man known as Metal-head said.

'Will I get a crown of laurel leaves?' Commodus asked.

'At least! Maybe the Emperor will give you a crown of silver... or gold!' the head of the gladiators' school sighed.

Commodus waved the short, sharp sword and Metal-head was glad he was wearing armour. 'Put the sword away!' he said quickly.

The boy slipped it back into his belt. 'So what do I have to do? Fight a Retarius with his net and his spear? I could fight ten of them! Twenty! I'd smash their spears to splinters! I'll shred their nets till they couldn't catch tiddlers!'

Metal-head held up a hand. 'You will not be fighting other men... you are too good. You would destroy them in a minute and the crowd would be bored!' the man lied smoothly.

'True,' Commodus agreed sadly.

'So we are going to set you against a ferocious animal!'

'A hippopobalus?'

'Hippopotamus?'

'Hippotoppermush!'

'No,' follow me.

Metal-head led the boy down the dark corridors of the amphitheatre. 'Phwoar! It stinks!' the Emperor's son cried.

'It's the smell of death, Commodus – a great gladiator like you must get used to that smell.'

'Oh, yes! I'll soon get used to it!' Commodus said with a light laugh.

Metal-head stepped into the lion house below the amphitheatre and grabbed a boy by the arm. 'You, slave!'

'I'm not a slave, sir,' Cass muttered. 'I'm the son of a free citizen.'

'Whatever... tell us which is the lion, Max?'

Cass nodded towards the cage. 'That's Max.'

Commodus ran to the bars and waved his sword. I'm going to kill you, lion! I'm going to chop your head off! I'm going to skin you and make you into a cloak! Hah! I'm not scared of you!'

Max glared then turned away.

'See!' Metal-head laughed. 'The sign of a true gladiator. Even a lion is afraid to face you! The crowd will love you, Commodus. The Christians will be driven in to the arena. They'll be attacked by the lion. We'll take you deep under the arena and place you under a trap door. As the lion heads for the Christians you will pop up in the middle like the hero Hercules! First you'll kill the lion –

and then you'll execute the Christians! Look…'

The Plan:

I: Lion enters

II: Christians enter

III: Gladiator enters

IV: Kills lion

V: Kills Christians

VI: Gladiator glorious

'This sketch will help you remember, Commodus.'

The Emperor's son nodded. 'Kill lion... chop – kill Christians. Choppety-chop-chop!'

'What?' Cass cut in. 'Hercules would never kill three defenceless people!'

Metellus turned on him savagely. 'There will be *four* defenceless people out there, slave, if you interrupt me again!'

'But the slave's right,' Commodus said.

'No!' the head of the gladiator school hissed. 'Those Christians may not be dangerous in their bodies. But their words and their lies are terrible! Kill them and save Rome from these cannibals!'

Commodus sighed. 'Perhaps, Metellus!'

The man grabbed the young gladiator by the throat. 'Look, boy, you may be the son of the Emperor but you gave up everything to be a gladiator. While you are a gladiator you obey me! I am your Emperor while you carry the gladius sword. Remember the gladiator vow?'

Commodus choked on the hand at his windpipe and recited, 'I will suffer being burned, being bound, being beaten and being killed by the sword!'

Metal-head released the boy and said, 'Never forget that vow.'

CHAPTER EIGHT
Diary of a goddess

Emperor Marcus Aurelius led the procession of gladiators around the arena while the crowds cheered and called for their favourites. The beak-nosed Verres walked a pace behind the Emperor and shouted over the din of the music and the cheering, 'The people love you, Emperor!'

Marcus Aurelius waved and muttered, 'I should hope they do. These games are costing me a fortune.'

It was as if his grumbling changed the mood of the crowd. The cheering faded, the trumpets played on and the gladiators marched around but no one was looking at them now. Just as Lucilla had expected, everyone turned to look at her as she took her place on one of the thrones at the edge of the arena wall. They stretched and twisted to see her under the striped silk canopy.

The Emperor's daughter raised her fan of peacock feathers to hide her face. The crowd sighed, the Emperor's daughter smirked. She turned to the slave beside her who held the writing materials and began to speak...

Here I am at the amphitheatre and the crowds adore me, as I knew they would! Father doesn't look too pleased, but I can't help that. This is such a great day, I will keep notes so I never forget it.

Father has finished his walk and joined me on the platform with our ten guards, that cruel-faced Verres and the ruffian Metallus. Here are gladiators they call andabatae. They are fitted with helmets, like the other gladiators, but there are no eye-holes in the front! It is like the game blind-man's buff we play at the palace! The andabatae stumble around and swing their swords and the crowd scream to tell them where to go. And sometimes they crash into their enemy and fall on their backsides. Sometimes they crash into the fence around the arena! That was so funny! I wish I'd been to these games before!

Now we have two animals in the arena together - a lion and a tiger. Oh, this is not so much fun. They snarl and circle and then they start to tear at one another. I thought they'd be handsome animals like I've seen in the paintings on the palace walls. But they are thin and matted and scarred and pitiful. The crowd is screaming more savagely than the creatures in the arena. I feel sick. I will leave. I will go below and see the criminals. I haven't seen a Christian before. Oh, the blood on the sand! Slaves are scattering fresh sand before the next fight between a bear and a bull.

I am in the dark passageways beneath the arena. A boy tells me the lion here is called Max. He showed me the cells where the Christians are held. There was a scrap of paper there. I picked it up. It was a letter from one of the prisoners to an attendant. It says she doesn't want to die and asks the boy to help her escape. I must look at this girl.

Strangely, the door was open. I asked the boy - his name is Cassius - but I didn't tell him I'm the Emperor's daughter. I asked him who had left the door open. He said his master, Ferox, had been the last to visit the prisoners.

The Christian girl who wrote the letter is a pitiful thing. Not much more than a mouthful for Max. I will not stay to watch her execution. I asked her to say the words "Jupiter is the true god."

She replied, "I can't, because it's not true." I said I'd see her life was spared if she would only say the Emperor is a god. She refused. The woman prisoner even said she wanted to die and the crazed old man started singing about being eaten by a lion.

It is close to noon now. I'll return to sit by my father. We will leave for lunch while the executions take place.

The boy Cassius bent to slide the bolts in the door.

"Your master left it open," I reminded him.

"Yes, lady," he said.

"Then it would be wrong of you to lock it shut," I said.

"Yes, lady."

"Is that all you can say?"

"Yes, lady."

The foolish boy had tears in his eyes as he slid the bolts again to leave the door open.

"Why didn't the Christians escape before we arrived?" I asked.

"Perhaps they didn't know Ferox had left the door open," he said.

I stepped back towards the door. "You Christians! I say! It seems the animal master has left your cell door open! He is a careless man."

Then I turned and left.

The boy Cassius was quite disgusting. He snatched my hand and kissed it! The dirt and blood of the animal house was on his hand. Still, it was washed clean by the tears that fell. For some strange reason I found that half of those tears were mine.

I have cried before today, when my father refused me a treat. I don't think I have ever cried for someone else's misery. I am sure a goddess should not behave like this. I will be strong now and return to the throne by my father.

As Lucilla left the dreary underground passages she stopped and looked at the leg of beef that lay on the floor where Ferox had dropped it. 'Your job is to care for the lion, Max?'

'Yes, my lady,' Cass replied.

'Then your job is to feed it?'

'I give it water but no food. Ferox says it hasn't been fed for the past three days.'

'Then I am ordering you to give it that beef.'

'Ferox would have me thrown to the other hungry lions,' the boy muttered.

'No. Ferox will not dare go against the orders of the Emperor's friend. I know the Emperor well. Do it.'

'You know the Emperor?' The boy said suddenly. 'Can you take him a message? An urgent message – warn him ...'

'I am *not* a messenger,' Lucilla said coldly.

'Sorry, lady,' he said.

She turned and walked away. Lucilla had missed the chance to save her father from the plotters' knives – Cass had missed a chance to save the Emperor. It could have been his last chance. Then again...

CHAPTER NINE
A Roman way to die

The Emperor Marcus Aurelius stretched and yawned. The sun was hot now and it had been a long morning. He turned to the hawk-faced Verres and sighed, 'Time for lunch, I think! Where is my daughter?'

'I'm not sure,' replied the man they called Vicious. 'Perhaps we should stay here a few minutes while we see where she's gone. He made a silent signal with his hand to Metellus. Metellus waved to Ferox, the animal keeper, who stood next to the guard at the bottom of the stairs. Ferox slipped down a further dark stairway, into the bowels of the amphitheatre.

In the cell below the three Christians looked at the open door. 'It's our chance,' Agnes breathed. 'Our chance to live.'

'I wanted to die,' Miriam sighed.

The girl looked at Balbus. 'It's up to you, Balbus. We need you to decide – and we need you to lead us through this maze if you do want us to go free.'

The old man looked at the girl. 'I don't mind dying... I've lived a long and happy life... but... but it would be a waste if you died, Agnes, child. I'll vote to escape. I'll lead you out.'

Miriam shrugged. 'God knows best,' she said. 'If he'd wanted us to die he wouldn't have left the door open, would he?'

Agnes smiled and squeezed the woman's hand. 'Thanks, Miriam. Lead on Balbus!'

The old man crept out into the corridor. The only sounds were restless animals and the distant baying of the crowd. He waved a withered hand and led them into the dim, dank depths. 'Turn right here, as I remember, then second on the left.'

After walking past a giraffe for the second time, Agnes whispered to Miriam, 'I'm sure he's lost!'

'Trust in God,' Miriam told her.

Balbus turned left again and came to a door. Through the faint gap round the edges they could see the brilliant daylight and smell the cleaner air. 'Freedom!' Agnes moaned. 'Thank you, God!'

Balbus lifted the latch and led the girl and the woman out.

Ferox hurried past the lion's cage, calling to Cass, 'Now, boy! Pick up your whip and drive that lion out into the arena!'

'Yes, Ferox.'

'Count to forty and then drive the Christians in after him.'

'Yes, Ferox.'

'That will give me time to get the gladiator onto the lifting trapdoor and shoot him up into the arena. Well, boy, get on with it... quickly, before the Emperor decides to leave for lunch!'

'Yes, Ferox.'

The head keeper was in such a hurry that he didn't notice the lion licking its bloody paws and washing its stained whiskers. He didn't see the splinters of crunched bone that lay on the floor of the cage.

Cass pulled a rope that opened the lion's cage door into the arena. Hot, fresh air and dazzling light flooded in to the animal house. Max blinked and yawned. Cass picked up a whip and prodded the lion gently. 'Come on, Max boy. Time to go.'

The lion struggled to its feet, its full belly stretched and heavy. It ambled towards the opening and memories of the African plains stirred it.

'Best of luck!' Cass called after it then closed the door. The boy hurried to the cells to see if the crazy Christians had taken their chance.

The cell door was wide open.

The cell was empty.

Cass gave a great grin and said aloud, 'Oh, dear! The Christians have escaped. Oh, dear! Who was the last man to go and see them? It was Ferox, I seem to remember! Poor Ferox.

I wonder what the punishment is for letting prisoners escape?'

The grin faded quickly.

'The plot on the Emperor's life!' The Christians had all been saved. The lion was too full to eat Commodus. If Cass could get up to the Emperor in time he might be able to stop the bodyguard deserting him! He turned and ran.

Balbus led Miriam and Agnes out into the sunlight. The door slammed shut behind them and locked them out. There was no latch on this side. Agnes and Miriam followed the old man, blinded for a few moments by the light after days in the dark cell.

Then they stopped and gazed in wonder. Fifty thousand pairs of eyes gazed back.

'Balbus,' Agnes groaned. 'You've led us into the arena!'

'It's God's will,' Miriam said happily. She marched towards the centre of the arena. A huge lion with a shabby mane had come from a nearby door. It flopped onto its side to doze on the sand in the hot midday sun. 'Right, lion! I am ready!' the woman cried.

Fifty thousand voices were hushed. In the silence one voice sang out – an old and tuneless voice that was joined by a frail girl's voice. Together they sang...

If you're listening lion,
We have a nice suggestion,
Don't you eat us Christians,
Or you'll get indigestion!

All things bright and wonderful,
We are your daily bread,
But if you eat us Christians,
You won't get to Heaven when you're dead.

The lion looked at the woman waving her skinny arms. It looked across at the withered man and the little girl who had their hands pressed together in prayer. They were making a dreadful wailing sound that could have been singing. The lion rose to its feet. Its tawny eyes were level with the woman's and its hot, stinking breath snorted over her face.

'Eat me!' she cried.

'Don't you eat us Christians!' Balbus sang.

Max the lion blinked, turned and shambled away to lie in the small patch of shade by the wall under the Emperor's seat.

There was a gasp from the crowd.

'A miracle!' Agnes cried.

'Our prayers must have worked!' Balbus roared as he rushed out to clasp Miriam in a tearful hug.

'I was looking forward to meeting God,' the woman sighed.

'A miracle!' the crowd muttered and the mutter became a roar.

Ferox arrived at the heart of the tunnels under the arena. He was panting slightly. 'Now, Commodus, are you ready?'

'I have my arm guard and my shield from the gladiator school, but I haven't got my sword and helmet.'

'No, I've got them here. Let me fasten this helmet onto your head,' he said and pushed it on quickly.

'By Jupiter, it's dark!' Commodus laughed. 'Hope it'll be a bit lighter up there!

'Not really,' Ferox said. 'I've given you one of the andabatae helmets.'

'I'll be fighting the lion blind!' Commodus said.

'You will.'

'Jupiter, that's hard,' Commodus said. 'But fun. And no problem for a hero!'

'Here's your sword,' Ferox said.

'It's light!'

'That's because it's a wooden practice sword!' Ferox said with a savage sort of happiness.

'Ohhh! That makes it really hard – I guess we have to give the old lion a chance, eh?'

'That's true, in fact the lion should finish you off in the beat of a butterfly's wing, Commodus the clown. Off you go, you stupid little son of an Emperor!'

Commodus was about to argue when Ferox hauled at a rope and sent the lift rattling upwards. A trapdoor opened and Commodus shot into the arena and landed in a cloud of sand.

All he could hear was the crowd roaring, 'Miracle!'

'Not really,' the boy grinned. 'Just a simple trick with the trapdoor. Now, lion… time to die! Lion? Here, pussy, pussy! Where are you? I'm coming to get you!'

CHAPTER TEN
Saving the Emperor

'Commodus!' Lucilla screamed at her father.

'What? Where?' the Emperor asked.

'In the arena! The gladiator is Commodus.'

'By Mars, it is! Just as well the lion's not hungry!' the Emperor sighed.

'No, Emperor,' Vicious Verres said, stepping alongside him. 'The lion won't eat the *Christians* because their God has saved them! But your son, Commodus, isn't a Christian. The lion *will* eat *him!*'

'Commodus can't see!' Lucilla cried.

'And he only has a wooden sword!' Verres added. He turned his hawk face on Metellus, the gladiator chief. 'What's wrong with that lion?' he hissed.

'Maybe that ferret Ferox has fed it and betrayed us! He'll die a hideous death if he has,' Metalhead spat.

Verres turned back to the Emperor. 'Quick, Emperor! You must rescue your son!'

'Me!' Marcus Aurelius squawked. 'I'm too old to go jumping into arenas, I'd probably get hurt! And my stomach-ache is bad today. I can't jump down there. I may be a god, I may live forever, but I don't want to live forever with a broken leg, thank you very much, Verres!'

'I meant, sir, you must send your bodyguards into the arena!' Verres said and signed for Metellus to be ready.

'Send my bodyguard?' the Emperor exploded. 'While my bodyguards are bodyguarding my son's body, then who'll bodyguard my body?'

'I will! And Metellus will!' Verres said smoothly. 'But act quickly before your son is torn to shreds before your very eyes!'

'He deserves it,' Lucilla snapped, 'but I suppose Verres is right. It wouldn't look good.'

The Emperor scowled and shrugged, 'Oh, very well, Verres... send my guard in to rescue him!'

Cass was having problems. He'd found his way up to the ground level of the amphitheatre but couldn't get up the dozen stairs to the first floor where the Emperor sat. 'More than my job's worth to let a common slave go up there!' the guard said. His helmet was a little too small for his fat head and it perched there, tilted slightly to one side.

'It's a matter of life and death!' Cass shouted.

'Yes, the Emperor's life and your death if you don't push off, sonny.'

'There's a hippopotamus loose in the animal house and it's coming up the stairs!' Cass lied desperately.

The guard narrowed his little black eyes. 'A hippo couldn't get up those stairs – it's too fat, sonny! I'm not as stupid as I look!'

'It's a very *thin* hippo,' Cass said. 'It's been starved so it's really hungry. It'll eat you – armour and all – then it'll run up the stairs and finish the Emperor off – toga and all!'

The guard gave a nervous laugh. 'Where's this hippo?' he asked.

Cass jabbed a finger in the direction of the dark stairs behind him. 'There!' The boy gasped. 'It's coming now! Can't you *see* it?'

The guard squinted towards the stairway and took a step forward to get a better look. 'There's nothing…'

That step forward was all Cass needed to slip past the man and race up the stairs to the sunlit platform with the Emperor's seats.

When he arrived he looked across the platform. The Emperor's bodyguards were jumping down into the arena to surround the lion and form a wall between Max and Commodus.

The crowd were getting excited by this new sport, especially when Commodus caught the sound of the guards' rattling armour and raced towards them. 'Die, you cowards, die!' he screamed and raced towards them waving his wooden sword.

The guards turned their backs on Max and tried to deal with the whirling, screaming boy without hurting him, while the crowd roared.

Just as they planned it, no one was watching the Emperor as Verres and Metellus drew daggers and pointed them at him. They had their backs to the arena. When Cass described it later he drew a sketch…

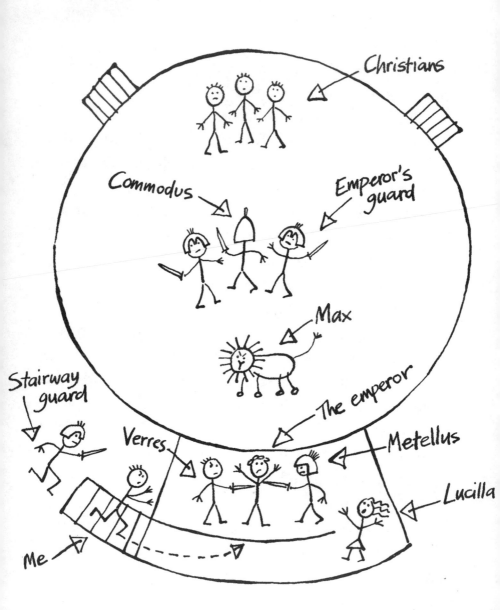

Lucilla was the only one watching the kidnap. She saw Cass at the top of the stairs and screamed. 'Cassius, boy! Help the Emperor!' No one heard her except Cass.

The stairway guard clattered up the stairs, sword drawn, calling, 'Hey, sonny! I said you can't come up here!'

He waved his sword at Cass, then saw what was happening behind the boy. His mouth fell open and his sword lowered.

Cass jumped at him, snatched the sword and turned. He raced past Lucilla, who shouted, 'Get them, Cassius!'

Metellus raised his dagger and snarled like the fiercest lion in the amphitheatre. He'd have carved Cassius to dormouse mince. But the cowardly Verres took a step back. The backs of his knees hit the bronze rail at edge of the arena. He was falling backwards. He snatched at the sword-belt of Metellus to save himself.

Metellus tried to free himself and pushed back. Verres tumbled over the edge of the arena wall and dragged Metellus with him.

The men may have survived the fall, who knows? But they landed on Max. The lion may not have been hungry, but finding himself sat on by two Romans made him very angry.

Very.

Max roused himself enough to destroy the two traitors in a flurry of flesh and flailing claws.

The bodyguard had finally got a hold of Commodus. They lifted him up to where his stunned father waited. Then they hauled themselves out of the arena and safely out of Max's reach. The arena sand was empty except for three wide-eyed Christians and a contented lion chewing on its grisly lunch.

The crowd applauded wildly and cheered the Emperor. 'Great entertainment!' they all agreed as they slipped out of their seats to have their lunch.

CHAPTER ELEVEN
The Emperor's new guard

The Emperor stretched a hand out towards Cass. 'You have saved the life of the Emperor of Rome.'

'He was wonderful,' Lucilla smiled.

Commodus looked hurt. 'I was pretty good myself, Sis! Blindfolded, with just a wooden sword and it took ten of your best guards to capture me!'

The Emperor sighed. 'Yes, my son, a brave fight. Now be silent while I think of a suitable reward for this slave.'

'I'm the son of a freedman,' Cass said humbly.

The Emperor shook his head. 'So I can't reward you with your freedom. What can I offer you?'

Cassius looked up and dared to meet the Emperor's eyes. 'Could I have the freedom of four others? Is that asking too much?'

The Emperor spread his hands. 'No, my boy. Who are they?'

Cass raised an arm and pointed to Agnes, Miriam and Balbus who were on their knees in the sun-baked sand, praying. 'The three Christians.'

The Emperor nodded. ''Granted. And the fourth?'

'Your executioner,' Cass said with a shy smile. 'Max the lion!'

The Emperor laughed. 'I think you are too soft-hearted to be an animal keeper in this place.'

Cass nodded. 'I am.'

'So perhaps you had better give up that job. I need two new bodyguards. Ones I can trust.'

'Me?' Cass asked.

'Of course!'

'And me!' Commodus put in.

The Emperor shook his head. 'No. I was thinking of Max. Who better to protect the Emperor of Rome than the king of the animals?'

So Cass and Max became the Emperor's bodyguards at the palace in Rome. And while the Emperor's two new guards protected him, you can be sure the Emperor of Rome was safe.

Author's Note

Most of the characters in the story are invented but the Flavian Amphitheatre and all its horrors were terribly real. It is now called the Colosseum and you can see the ruins in Rome.

The Emperor, Marcus Aurelius, lived from AD 121 till AD 180. He is remembered as one of Rome's greatest Emperors... but still enjoyed the gruesome games. The Emperor didn't like Christians and was happy to see them executed when they were caught, but he didn't seek them out to destroy them.

Commodus, the son of Marcus Aurelius (born AD 161) grew up to be a very strange man but was still allowed to become Emperor when his father died. Commodus insisted on being allowed to fight in the amphitheatres of Rome. Commodus really believed he was Hercules going to fight lions with arrows. He slaughtered thousands of animals – of course the animal keepers and rival gladiators made sure he always won. He spent so much time in the arena he was a weak Emperor and very unpopular.

After he'd ruled for just two years there was a revolt against Commodus. The chief plotter? His sister, Lucilla. The plot failed, but ten years later another plot succeeded and Commodus was murdered in his bath.

In time the Emperors of Rome became Christians themselves and their sickening executions stopped.

The blood on the sand has long since dried and been swept away. But the memories of the dreadful days of death in the sun should live on forever.